BIG PIG'S HAT

Dial Books for Young Readers
New York

BIG PIG'S HAT

STORY BY WILLY SMAX

PICTURES BY KEREN LUDLOW

TO TOM AND JOSH

First published in the United States 1993 by
Dial Books for Young Readers
A Division of Penguin Books USA Inc.
375 Hudson Street
New York, New York 10014

Published in Great Britain 1992 by Orchard Books
Text copyright © 1992 by Willy Smax
Pictures copyright © 1992 by Keren Ludlow
All rights reserved · Printed in Belgium
First Edition
10 9 8 7 6 5 4 3 2 1

Library of Congress Cataloging in Publication Data
Smax, Willy.
Big Pig's hat / story by Willy Smax
pictures by Keren Ludlow.—1st ed.
p.   cm.
Summary: There's trouble brewing in the town
of Beansville when Big Pig loses his hat.
ISBN 0-8037-1476-9
[1. Animals—Fiction. 2. Hats—Fiction.]
I. Ludlow, Keren, ill.   II. Title.
PZ7.S63934Bi 1993 [E]—dc20 92-19442 CIP AC

One night a great wind blew through
Beansville, U.S.A.

Lots of things got blown away.

Big Pig's house on the hill shivered and shook all night long.

In the morning Big Pig couldn't find his hat.

"Somebody's stolen my hat," he said. "Wait till I find out who."

Big Pig walked out into the bright street.
The Beansville folks saw him coming. There
was Slippy Snake the Deputy, Calamity Cat,

Mousey Mousey the Mechanic, and Coco
the Cow. "Look out," said Happy Horsey, "Big
Pig's a-comin' and boy, does he look mad!"

"Big Pig's got his boots on," said Slippy Snake.

"And his red bandanna," said Calamity Cat.

"And he's wearing his pistols," squeaked Mousey Mousey.

"But no hat," said Coco the Cow. "Maybe he lost it."

"Who's got my hat?" shouted Big Pig.
Nobody said nothin'.

"Here comes Dirty Donkey," said Happy Horsey. "Maybe he knows where it is."

"He don't know," said Big Pig. "I'm off to find out who's got my hat — out of my way."

And he pushed Dirty Donkey down.

Dirty Donkey sat in the dust. He watched Big Pig go.

Just then a gust of wind blew Big Pig's hat over a roof and right down in front of him.

Dirty Donkey got up
even dirtier than
he was before.
He picked up Big Pig's
hat and put it on.

"Uh-oh," said
Happy Horsey.
"What does Dirty Donkey
think he's doing?"

"Big Pig's coming back — there sure is going to be trouble now!" Calamity Cat called out.

Everybody tried to hide.

Mousey Mousey
ran up
a drainpipe.

Slippy Snake
slipped into
a slipper.

Happy Horsey
hid in
a barrel.

Coco the Cow
cowered
in a corner.

"Give me back my hat," shouted Big Pig.
"Nope," said Dirty Donkey.

"If you don't give me back my hat,
I'll get you," yelled Big Pig.

"Go ahead. See if I care," said Dirty
Donkey.

Big Pig's trotters went for his pistols.

Dirty Donkey just stood there, waiting.

"I can't look," said Happy Horsey, and he covered his eyes to prove it.

Big Pig squirted Dirty Donkey.

SPLOOSH!

Dirty Donkey stood in the middle of a big muddy puddle.

"Well, just look at that," said Slippy Snake from his slipper. "Dirty Donkey is all clean!"

Dirty Donkey looked pleased.

"Thank you kindly, Big Pig. I've been needing a wash for weeks. Here, you can have your hat back now."

Big Pig took his hat from Dirty Donkey.
He looked mighty happy – until he put it on.
"Ugh! It's all wet!" he said.

Off went Big Pig with water from his wet hat dripping down his neck.

How the Beansville folks laughed as they watched him go!

Now everybody looked at Dirty Donkey.

"Dirty Donkey, you're not dirty anymore," said Mousey Mousey.

"You're so brave," said Coco the Cow.

"Big Pig won't push you around again in a hurry," said Slippy Snake.

And you can be sure that he didn't.